GUMSHOE GOOSE
PRIVATE EYE

by Mary DeBall Kwitz
pictures by Lisa Campbell Ernst

PUFFIN BOOKS

For Kendra

M. K.

.

PUFFIN BOOKS
Published by the Penguin Group
Penguin Books USA Inc., 375 Hudson Street, New York, New York 10014, U.S.A.
Penguin Books Ltd, 27 Wrights Lane, London W8 5TZ, England
Penguin Books Australia Ltd, Ringwood, Victoria, Australia
Penguin Books Canada Ltd, 10 Alcorn Avenue, Toronto, Ontario, Canada M4V 3B2
Penguin Books (N.Z.) Ltd, 182-190 Wairau Road, Auckland 10, New Zealand

Penguin Books Ltd, Registered Offices: Harmondsworth, Middlesex, England

First published in the United States of America by Dial,
a division of Penguin Books USA Inc., 1988
Published in a Puffin Easy-to-Read edition, 1996

3 5 7 9 10 8 6 4 2

Text copyright © Mary DeBall Kwitz, 1988
Illustrations copyright © Lisa Campbell Ernst, 1988
All rights reserved

THE LIBRARY OF CONGRESS HAS CATALOGED THE DIAL EDITION AS FOLLOWS:
Kwitz, Mary DeBall. Gumshoe Goose, private eye.
Summary: Detective Gumshoe Goose helps his father,
Inspector Goose, solve the case of the hungry kidnapper.
[1. Mystery and detective stories. 2. Geese—Fiction.]
I. Ernst, Lisa Campbell, ill. II. Title.
PZ7.K976Gu   1988   [E]   86-29331
W
ISBN 0-8037-0423-2

Puffin Books ISBN 0-14-036194-4

Puffin® and Easy-to-Read® are registered trademarks of Penguin Books USA Inc.
Printed in the United States of America

Reading Level 2.1

Contents

Private Eye at Work

Gumshoe Goose, the ace detective,
was sitting in his office.
He was polishing his spyglass.
"Business is slow today," he said.
"I'll telephone my father,
Inspector Goose, at the jail.
Maybe he can use some help."

"Hello, Father," said Gumshoe.

"This is your son, G. Goose,

the ace detective."

"Who?" asked Inspector Goose.

"Your son, Gumshoe,"

said Gumshoe Goose.

"Stop playing detective,

Gumshoe," said his father.

"Get yourself a real job."

"This *is* my real job,"

said Gumshoe Goose.

"But I am not busy today.

Can I help you solve a crime?"

"No," said Inspector Goose.

"But watch out for Fat Fox,

Public Enemy Number One.

There is always trouble

when he comes to town."

Gumshoe looked out the window.

Fat Fox was nowhere in sight.

"Looking for Public Enemy Number One
makes my eyes tired," he said.

Gumshoe yawned.

Then he leaned back

in his chair.

He put his feet up on the desk

and closed his eyes.

Zzzzzzz, snored Gumshoe Goose.

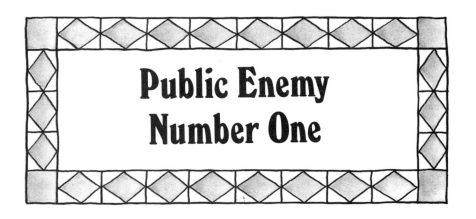

Public Enemy
Number One

Fat Fox was hungry.

"Granny," he said,

"where is my breakfast?"

"I can't see," said Granny Fox.

"I have lost my glasses.

I can't cook until I find them."

"They are on your forehead,"
said Fat Fox.

"Oh, deary me!" cried Granny.
She pulled down her glasses
and set about making breakfast.

Fat Fox ate everything

on his plate.

"That tasted *great*!"

he said.

"What was it, Granny?"

"Fried worms on toast,"

said Granny Fox.

"Yuck!" muttered Fat Fox.

"What's for lunch?" he asked.

"Snake stew with lizard dumplings,"

said Granny.

"Double yuck!" growled Fat Fox.

14

"What we need around here
is some decent grub," he said.
"I'm going to town to get
something good for our dinner."
"While you are gone I think
I will take a nap," said Granny.
Fat Fox smiled his foxy smile.

15

When Granny fell asleep, Fat Fox took
off her glasses and put them on.
Then he put on her shawl and
took her shopping basket.

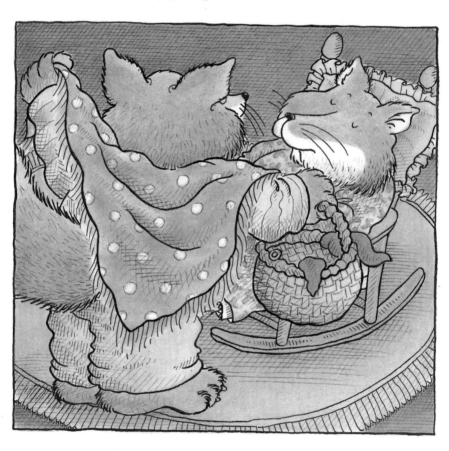

Fat Fox sang a cheery tune as
he started off to town.

"Chicken for breakfast,

Chicken for lunch.

Chicken anytime

Is great to munch," he sang.

17

Suddenly he saw Mrs. Hen coming
down the road.

Fat Fox jumped behind a bush.

Mrs. Hen went into the bakery.

Fat Fox listened at the door.

"I would like to buy a chocolate
birthday cake," said Mrs. Hen.

"It is for Baby Chick-Chick.

He is one month old today."

Fat Fox's mouth began to water.

"Chicken and dumplings,

Chicken and rice.

Little Baby Chick-Chick

Will taste very nice!" he whispered.

Inspector Goose came out of the jail.

"Good morning, Granny Fox," he said.

"Where is Fat Fox today?"

"Sleeping late," said Fat Fox

in his old granny voice.

Then he hurried down the road.

Fat Fox peeked in

Gumshoe Goose's window.

Gumshoe was taking a nap.

"This is my lucky day!" cried Fat Fox.

"Fried chicken,

Chicken in the pot.

Stewed Baby Chick-Chick,

Get it while it's hot!" he sang.

Then he ran down the road and
knocked on the henhouse door.

"Go away!" yelled Baby Chick-Chick.
"I'm not allowed to open
the door to strangers."

"It's Granny Fox," said Fat Fox

in his old granny voice.

"I have a birthday surprise for you."

Baby Chick-Chick opened the door

and Fat Fox stepped inside.

"Where is my birthday surprise?"
asked Baby Chick-Chick.

"SURPRISE!" yelled Fat Fox.

He popped Baby Chick-Chick into
the basket and closed the lid.

Fat Fox started to make his getaway.

Suddenly he thought of the cake.

"What a waste," said Fat Fox.

He loved chocolate cake almost

as much as chicken.

Fat Fox smiled his foxy smile.

"Maybe I can have the cake and

Baby Chick-Chick too," he said.

Fat Fox sat down at the table
and took off Granny's glasses.
He wrote a note to Mrs. Hen.
Just then Fat Fox heard Mrs. Hen
coming up the walk.

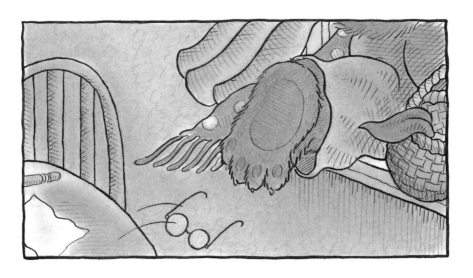

He grabbed the shopping basket
and jumped out the window.
He ran across a field and into
the woods to Granny's house.

28

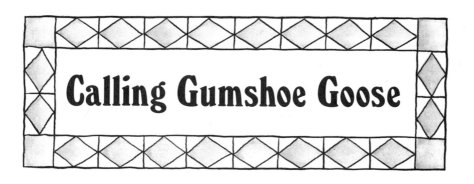

Calling Gumshoe Goose

"Wake up, Gumshoe Goose!"
yelled Mrs. Hen.

"Who's sleeping?" said Gumshoe.

"I was just resting my eyes."

"Baby Chick-Chick has been

kidnapped," cried Mrs. Hen.

"What shall I do, Gumshoe Goose?"

Gumshoe Goose stood up and bowed.
He was not only an ace detective
—he was a goose with good manners.

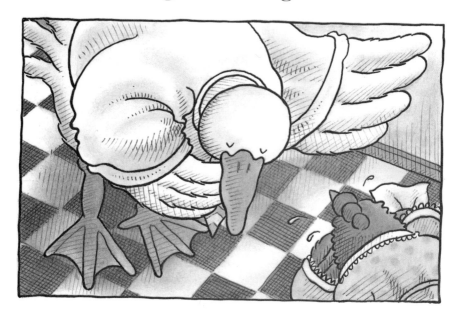

"What happened?" he asked.
"Well," said Mrs. Hen, crying,
"I left Baby Chick-Chick at home
while I went shopping.

"Then I went to the bakery

to buy a chocolate cake."

"Please," sighed Gumshoe,

"just give me the facts."

"These are the facts," she said.

"When I came home with the cake,

Baby Chick-Chick was gone.

I found this note on my table."

"Hmmmm," said Gumshoe Goose.

"Very interesting.

G. Goose will take the case."

Gumshoe telephoned the jail.

"Father," he said, "I am working
on a kidnapping case."

"Gumshoe," said Inspector Goose,
"that is police work."

"Right, Father," said Gumshoe.

"Meet me at the henhouse."

34

The Case of the Hungry Kidnapper

"Is this the scene of the crime?"

asked Inspector Goose at the henhouse.

"Yes," said Gumshoe Goose.

"I am calling this the Case of

the Hungry Kidnapper!"

"What does food have to do with

this case?" asked the Inspector.

Gumshoe handed him the note.

Mrs. Hen,
Leave the chocolate cake under the old oak tree tonight – or else Baby Chick-Chick will be in a chicken sandwich tomorrow.

"Don't worry, Mrs. Hen,"

said Inspector Goose.

"I will catch the kidnapper."

He ran back to the jail to get

his handcuffs.

Gumshoe Goose wrote in his black book:

Clue Number One: open window.

Clue Number Two: chocolate cake.

Inspector Goose came back with
the handcuffs.

"Where is Gumshoe?" he asked.

"Under the table," said Mrs. Hen.

"Son," yelled Inspector Goose,

"why are you under the table?"

"I'm looking for Clue Number Three,"

said Gumshoe.

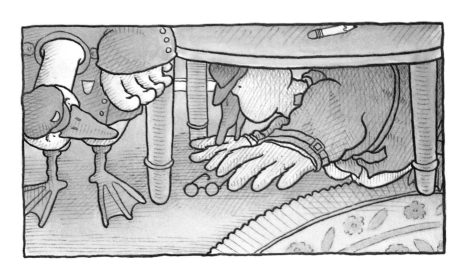

"Stop looking for clues,"
said Inspector Goose.

"I have cracked this case.

Granny Fox is the kidnapper.

I saw her come into town.

Follow me!" he cried.

Gumshoe and Mrs. Hen followed the
Inspector to Granny Fox's house.

They burst through the door.

Granny was asleep in her rocker.

Baby Chick-Chick was on the stove.

Fat Fox was adding salt and pepper.

"Ah-choo!" sneezed Baby Chick-Chick.

"My baby!" cried Mrs. Hen.

"Wake up, Granny, you are under arrest!"
yelled Inspector Goose.

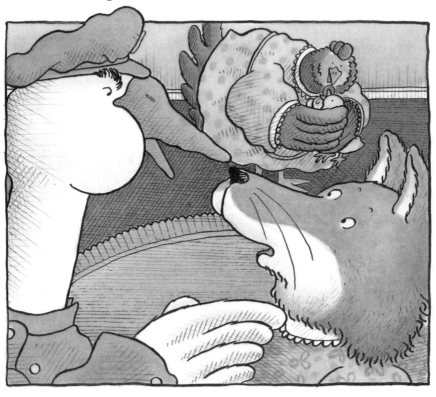

"Wait, Father," said Gumshoe,

"you have the wrong fox."

"Don't argue," said his father.

"I watched the road all day.

Only Granny came into town."

"Wrong, Father," said Gumshoe.

"It only looked like Granny.

You saw Fat Fox disguised as Granny."

"Prove it," said Fat Fox.

"Very simple," said Gumshoe.

He took Clue Number Three

out of his pocket.

"I found these glasses in the

henhouse," he said.

"They're Granny Fox's.

And Granny can't see without them.

So she wouldn't have left them

at the scene of the crime.

You made one mistake, Fat Fox.

You dropped Granny's glasses

when you made your getaway."

"Curses!" growled Fat Fox.

"Good work, Gumshoe!"

said Inspector Goose.

"I have caught the kidnapper!

The next time I need help,

I will call on you."

The Inspector locked up Fat Fox.

"What's for dinner?" asked Fat Fox.

"Bread and water,"

said Inspector Goose.

"Double curses!" growled Fat Fox.

Gumshoe Goose went to his office.

He opened his black book to

the Case of the Hungry Kidnapper.

Then he wrote: CASE CLOSED.

"Catching kidnappers is hard

work," he said.

"I think I will rest my eyes."

Zzzzzzzz, snored Gumshoe Goose.